KIDS'

WHODUNITS:

CATCH THE CLUES!

Blood-curdling mysteries by **HY CONRAD**

Shocking illustrations by **SUE BLANCHARD**

STERLING

New York / London

www.sterlingpublishing.com/kids

Dedicated to:

RYAN CASEY,

THE REAL INSPIRATION BEHIND THE FICTIONAL JONAH

STERLING and the distinctive Sterling logo are registered trademarks of
Sterling Publishing Co., Inc.

Library of Congress Cataloging-in-Publication Data

Conrad, Hy.
  Kids' whodunits : catch the clues! / Hy Conrad ; illustrated by Susan Blanchard.
    p. cm.
  Includes index.
  ISBN-13: 978-1-4027-3966-8
  ISBN-10: 1-4027-3966-4
  1. Puzzles--Juvenile literature. 2. Detective and mystery stories--Juvenile literature. I. Blanchard,
Susan, ill. II. Title.

GV1507.D4C6673 2007
793.73--dc22

2007017625

2 4 6 8 10 9 7 5 3

Published by Sterling Publishing Co., Inc.
387 Park Avenue South, New York, NY 10016
© 2007 by Hy Conrad
Distributed in Canada by Sterling Publishing
c/o Canadian Manda Group, 165 Dufferin Street
Toronto, Ontario, Canada M6K 3H6
Distributed in the United Kingdom by GMC Distribution Services
Castle Place, 166 High Street, Lewes, East Sussex, England BN7 1XU
Distributed in Australia by Capricorn Link (Australia) Pty. Ltd.
P.O. Box 704, Windsor, NSW 2756, Australia

Manufactured in the United States of America
All rights reserved

Sterling ISBN-13: 978-1-4027-3966-8
ISBN-10: 1-4027-3966-4

Designed by Lauren Rille

For information about custom editions, special sales, premium and
corporate purchases, please contact Sterling Special Sales
Department at 800-805-5489 or specialsales@sterlingpub.com.

CONTENTS

INTRODUCTION

JONAH BIXBY WAS NOT your average twelve-year-old. He spent more time in police stations than most career criminals. And although he had just started middle school, Jonah was single-handedly responsible for bringing more than a few of those career criminals to justice. But let's start at the beginning....

Jonah's mother and his father had both been police detectives in the city's Major Crimes Division, solving murders and assaults and high-profile robberies. It was while working there that they met and fell in love, then got married and had a son.

When Jonah was only five, his father was killed in the line of duty. At that point, Carol Bixby could have retired from the force. But she didn't. She stayed busy with the most important job she knew, law enforcement. And that's how young Jonah became the unofficial mascot of the Beaverton Police Department.

From the first grade on, Jonah would get out of school each day, walk across the street to the Fifth Precinct, and wait until his mother got off her shift. Carol's fellow officers took turns keeping an eye on him. Detective Massey from the Fraud Squad helped young Jonah with his math homework, while Sergeant Gonzales tutored him in Spanish.

Jonah was blessed with an inquisitive mind and an eye for detail. And his love for police work came naturally. Before long, he was making deductions even the best officers on the force couldn't come up with and whispering them to his mother. Little did the other detectives know that many of Detective Bixby's toughest crimes were being solved by her preteen son.

THE HAUNTED TREE HOUSE

FOR JONAH AND HIS FRIENDS, the one sure sign of spring was the opening of the tree house. It had been built in the fork of a huge oak in the Smiths' backyard. For the past four summers, Sally Smith, Bill Tollbar, Lisa Valdez, and Jonah had convened there almost daily to play games and talk and eat lunch. They used to call it the Oak Tree Club, but now that they were twelve, they were too cool for a club. Although Jonah didn't want to think of it, this would probably be their last summer before turning the tree house over to Sally's younger brother and his friends.

On a warm Saturday in late April, Sally got the key from her mother and, with Jonah and the others, climbed the ladder and unlocked the padlock that had kept the clubhouse secure through the long winter months.

The tree house was just one room, with the tree trunk and a large limb poking through the floor and dissecting the space. The structure was solid but far from weatherproof. As the kids unlatched and opened the shutters, they could feel the musty dampness. Anything made of metal, like the telescope stand, was a little rusty, and tiny pools of water near the trunk spoke of last week's torrential rains.

Jonah and Bill took the job of sweeping it out, while Sally and Lisa did general cleaning. "Oh, my gosh," said Sally. She was pointing to something on the other side of the room. "Look!"

The boys joined them and saw it, too. There, on the wall, were five words written in blood-red paint: "Welcome Back, Children.—The Specter."

The Specter was their own creation, a bogeyman they invented last Halloween, right before closing the tree house. Jonah had started the story of an angry tree spirit who seeps through the walls and curses them all. Sally took up the story next, and by the end of the evening, they had managed to scare each other pretty thoroughly.

The four of them stared at the scrawled words, open-mouthed. And then Bill laughed. "Good job, Sal. You had us going there."

"It wasn't me," Sally protested. "I haven't been up here since we locked up. My mom's had the key ever since. Go ask her."

"You probably know where she keeps it," said Bill.

"I don't," said Sally. "I haven't been up here at all. I swear."

"Did you guys tell anyone else about the Specter?" asked Jonah. They all shook their heads. "Then it had to be one of us."

"Right," said Sally. "One of you guys. You could have sneaked in, probably some day when my family and I were away."

Bill bristled at the accusation. "And how did we get in without a key?"

"Wait a minute," said Jonah. "Isn't there a spare key to the padlock?"

"Right. I hid it inside the tree house. Up there," Sally said, pointing to the ledge above a window. "Last Halloween, one of you must have taken it, just so you could pull this prank."

"That's easy to check," said Lisa as she hopped up on a chair and brushed her hand over the ledge. A few seconds of brushing and the spare key came falling to the floor.

They all stared at the bright, shiny key. Silently, Sally picked it up and tried it in the padlock. It worked.

Lisa got down from the table, her face white. "So, if Sal didn't do it, and if the spare key was inside the tree house all along..."

Three of the kids shivered. Could the Specter be for real? But Jonah wasn't shivering like the others. He was laughing.

WHO WROTE THE MYSTERIOUS MESSAGE?
HOW DID JONAH KNOW?

TURN TO PAGE 80 FOR THE SOLUTION TO "THE HAUNTED TREE HOUSE."

DETECTIVE PETER PAULING glanced up from his paperwork and was surprised to see a boy with a backpack standing in front of his desk. "Jonah! Hi." He checked a nearby wall clock. "Is it six o'clock already? How was band practice?"

"Pretty good," said Jonah. "Is my mom around?"

Jonah Bixby's school was directly across from the Beaverton Police Station, and nearly every day Jonah waved hello to the desk sergeant and made his way back to the Major Crimes Division bullpen to wait for his mother.

"Carol's at a crime scene," the middle-aged detective told him. "I have to get over there myself. You want to come?"

A few minutes later, Jonah was in the passenger seat of a police cruiser as they pulled up in front of Clawson & Wolfe Jewelry, an expensive shop in the downtown district. The seventh-grader expected to be told to wait in the car, but Detective Pauling didn't say a word, and Jonah wound up following him past the yellow crime tape, through the jewelry showroom, and into a rear storage room. The first thing he noticed was the blood.

Against the far wall of the room stood a floor safe, about four feet square, its door flung open. All around the safe was blood, drops of it on the floor and streaks of it across the back wall. In contrast, the inside of the safe was as clean as a whistle, without blood and without a trace of the trays of gems that were usually stored there.

The next thing Jonah Bixby noticed was the source of the blood, a tall heavyset man sprawled a few feet in front of the safe. A crime-scene technician knelt over the body, taking swabs from under his fingernails, while another took dozens of photographs, recording the blood spatter patterns on the floor and walls and on the door to the huge safe.

Detective Carol Bixby was off to one side, away from the blood, questioning a man and a woman. The woman still had a look of horror on her face. From his mother's questions, Jonah deduced that this was Madelyn Wolfe, co-owner of Clawson & Wolfe. Her partner, Otto Clawson, had been the victim.

"It was shortly after five P.M.," Miss Wolfe stammered. "Otto and I had just put the inventory into the safe and locked it when the front bell rang. It was a man with a large box in his arms, like a deliveryman. It was only after Otto had opened the door that we saw..." She shuddered at the memory. "He was wearing a ski mask and had a gun."

"Did you recognize his voice?" asked Carol.

"He didn't say much," Miss Wolfe replied. "He forced me into that closet and locked me in. Then I heard him talking to Otto. I kept yelling, 'Otto, open the safe. It's not worth getting killed for.' A minute or so later, I heard the shot."

Madelyn Wolfe paused to take a deep breath, which finally gave the other witness a chance to speak. "I guess I'm the one who discovered the body." His name was Gilbert Green and he was the dead man's next-door neighbor.

"Otto's car is in the shop," he continued, "so he asked me to pick him up after work. I got here around 5:30 and found the front door open. I heard a woman screaming, so I came back here and saw this." He stopped and scanned the room, just to make sure. "Except Madelyn was locked in the closet. I didn't want to touch anything, so I dialed 911 on my cell. It was your men who broke down the closet door."

Detective Bixby nodded, but her mind was elsewhere. Something didn't make sense. "If Mr. Clawson opened the safe for the thief, like he was told," she muttered, "then why did the guy shoot him?"

"Maybe Clawson recognized his voice," suggested Detective Pauling. "Or maybe they fought over the gun."

"Maybe," Carol said, then at long last noticed her son standing in the doorway. "Jonah? What are you…" She turned angrily to Pauling. "You brought a twelve-year-old to an active murder scene? What were you thinking?"

Detective Pauling shrugged. "He's been to murder scenes before."

But Carol was already at the door, ushering Jonah away from the blood-filled room. "Sorry about this, kiddo. Did you get anything to eat? I'll get a patrolman to take you out for a burger."

"I'm not hungry," Jonah protested. "Mom, one of them is lying. I think one of them killed Mr. Clawson."

WHOM DOES JONAH SUSPECT OF MURDER?
WHAT MADE JONAH SUSPICIOUS?

TURN TO PAGE 80 FOR THE SOLUTION TO "AFTER-SCHOOL HOMICIDE."

CRAZY KATE

IT WAS SATURDAY, and for Jonah that meant a visit to Crazy Kate. Every Saturday, his mother would put together a few bags of groceries and have Jonah and his friends deliver them to the old woman who lived in the shack across from the park. "At least once a week I know she gets some decent food," Carol Bixby said. "I feel sorry for the helpless old woman."

But Jonah and his friends knew Crazy Kate wasn't helpless. They knew you had to stop outside the gate to her overgrown yard and get her permission to enter. If you were dumb enough to open the gate without asking, Crazy Kate would hear you. Then a shotgun would appear at the window and a volley of birdseed would fly in your general direction.

"Hello!" called out Frankie. They had just parked their bikes outside the gate. "It's just us, Frankie, Bill, and Jonah. Can we come in?"

"All right," a voice called back. "Just the three of you, no one else."

A minute later and they were inside the shack, watching the old woman rummage through the bags. "Humph, the food was better last week," she complained. But that's exactly what she said every week. "You boys want to see something?" Before they could answer, Kate reached into a pile of newspapers and pulled out an old baseball. Bill examined the faded signature and let out a low whistle. "Babe Ruth! Wow!"

Kate smiled through her stained teeth. "My brother got it signed personally when he was a kid."

All the way home, the boys talked about the rare autographed ball. They talked about it again the next afternoon, when all three ran into each other at the skateboard ramp in the park. "Can you believe she's got something like that in the middle of all that junk?" Frankie said, pointing to the shack across the street. "What a waste."

Jonah followed his gaze to Crazy Kate's shack, then suddenly noticed something. "Look at the window," he said. "It's broken."

"I thought she always had a broken window," said Bill.

"No, it wasn't broken yesterday. I wonder if something's wrong."

Jonah and Bill argued about what to do. Should they just forget about it? Or should they check on Kate and make sure she was all right. Or should they…Jonah turned around to get Frankie's opinion, but he wasn't there.

"Hey, guys." Frankie was already at Kate's front door, peering inside. "I don't think she's home."

Jonah and Bill joined Frankie at the door. "Miss Kate?" Jonah called out as he knocked. "Are you there?"

"No, I'm not," came the angry reply. The three boys spun in their tracks just in time to see Crazy Kate barreling up the walkway. "I know what you hooligans are up to," she spat. "You're trying to steal my baseball."

The disheveled woman rushed past them and into the shack. "No! It's gone," she gasped. She was already on her hands and knees, pawing through the old newspapers. The baseball wasn't anywhere in sight.

"Thieves! You lure me out of my house, and then you break in and steal my baseball."

"Lure you out?" Jonah said. "Who lured you out? What happened?"

Crazy Kate scowled as she told her story. Half an hour ago, she received a phone call. "It sounded like a woman, but it could've been a boy. The voice said I just inherited some money. I went out to meet that person at the diner, but no one came. That's when you stole my ball."

"No," Bill swore. "We saw the broken window, and we came to see if you were all right. We didn't steal anything."

"You're lying. No one else knew about that baseball, just you kids."

"I know what must've happened," said Frankie with a smile.

"So do I," thought Jonah. And he wasn't smiling.

WHO STOLE THE BASEBALL?
WHAT CLUE DID JONAH NOTICE?
TURN TO PAGE 81 FOR THE SOLUTION TO "CRAZY KATE."

THE GENIE, THE MOVIE STAR, AND THE HOBO

DETECTIVE BIXBY PICKED her son up from school, waving him quickly into the car. "We just got an anonymous tip," Carol Bixby said as she pulled away from the curb. "The Diamond Expo is going to be robbed today."

Jonah had been looking forward to going home to his usual after-school snack, but this was even better. "Diamond Expo? Isn't that at the Hotel Royale?"

"Right, as always," Ms. Bixby said as she turned down First Street. "The tip says Margo the Cat will be involved. No one knows what she looks like, so we're blanketing the hotel with undercover officers."

She parked at a broken meter and whisked her son into the hotel lobby. "You stay here," she ordered as they passed the hotel shop. "And try to stay out of trouble. This case is for grown-ups."

Jonah did as he was told, but kept his eyes peeled. What caught his attention first was not a woman but a man, burly and bald, like a genie in a fairy tale. The genie was loitering in the hotel lobby's shop. Eventually he bought a bottle of aspirin, foot powder, and a pack of anti-snoring strips.

Right next to the shop was the hotel's jewelry store. Jonah saw a man in there, perfectly dressed and movie-star handsome.

He was browsing the display cases, even though the Diamond Expo, a hundred feet away, contained many more interesting samples.

The third suspect resembled a street person. His tousled hair and scruffy whiskers reminded Jonah of the hobos he'd seen in old photographs. The man was circling the lobby's flower arrangements, smelling the roses, and looking over his shoulder.

It was at about this time that Jonah wandered into the shop and became distracted by a mystery novel in the book rack. He picked it up, read the jacket blurb, examined the cover illustration, and was convinced that he'd figured out the ending....And then the lights went out.

Three minutes later, when the hotel's power came back on, his mother had rejoined him. Things were bad. Despite the police presence, Margo had struck again, using the darkness and the failure of the alarm system to get away with two million dollars' worth of gems.

Detective Bixby blamed herself. "We knew Margo had just gotten married, so we should have known she'd have an accomplice. There's a power closet right in the lobby. Her husband must have slipped in and cut the lines."

Jonah described the three suspicious-looking men. "Maybe one of them is her husband," he suggested. All three were brought over for questioning.

The genie's name was Alfred Kingsley. He claimed to be a bachelor, living alone in the suburbs. "I drove in to see the Expo, then bought a few things I'd been meaning to pick up."

The movie star was Cliff McCaskey, a salesman who worked at one of the Expo's jewelry booths. "I was just on a break," he told them. "Out of curiosity, I stepped into the jewelry shop. The stuff at my booth was much better."

The hobo claimed to be homeless and was carrying no I.D. "My name is Homer Gates. I came in to get out of the cold. I hung out by the flowers, hoping to grab a few and sell them on the street."

Jonah listened to all three stories, then whispered to his mother. "That man is lying," he said, pointing at one of them. I think he's Margo's husband."

WHO WAS JONAH POINTING AT?
WHAT WAS THE MAN LYING ABOUT?

TURN TO PAGE 81 FOR THE SOLUTION TO
"THE GENIE, THE MOVIE STAR, AND THE HOBO."

AUNT PENNY'S BROOCH

IT WAS A FRIGID DAY in February as Carol Bixby warmed herself in front of the fireplace in Aunt Penny's old-fashioned living room. Sitting beside her were her cousins, Aunt Penny's two other nieces. All of them stared silently at the Victorian brooch lying on a footstool, its central diamond gleaming in the fire's red glow.

Aunt Penny had died two weeks ago. On the afternoon after the funeral, her three nieces cleaned out the old woman's house. It was Stephanie who found the brooch in a dusty jewelry box in the attic. Her sister Gwen thought it must be a piece of cheap costume jewelry, but the other two cousins noticed the diamond's deep gleam. Together, they took it to a jeweler who confirmed their suspicions. It was real, all right. Aunt Penny's gaudy piece of jewelry was worth a lot.

The next day, their discovery made the local paper, complete with a color photo of the brooch. But all the publicity made Carol Bixby nervous. "We should get it insured," the police detective told her cousins. They both agreed, and that's what they were doing here on the coldest day of the year, waiting for the insurance appraiser to arrive and place a value on it.

Jonah walked in from the kitchen, munching a PB&J sandwich, just in time to see Stephanie picking up the brooch and cupping it in her hands. "You know, I'm the one who found this," she said. "It's rightfully mine."

"Don't start that," Gwen said. "Aunt Penny left her estate to all of us. We'll sell it and divide the proceeds."

Gwen grabbed the brooch from her sister. Then Stephanie tried to grab it back. It looked to Jonah like a fight might break out right then and there. But that's when the doorbell rang.

A half-frozen man in an overcoat stood on the porch. "John Bitterman," he announced, showing them his card. "Apex Fine Insurables. May I come in?"

The three women ushered him inside and took his coat. Carol offered him a chair, and Stephanie ran off to the kitchen to pour him a cup of coffee.

"I suppose you want to see the brooch," Gwen said and handed it to the stocky middle-aged man.

John Bitterman adjusted the floor lamp, took a jeweler's loupe from his pocket, and began to inspect the central diamond. He turned it over, then put it back on the table. "I hate to be the one to tell you, but this brooch is a fake."

Stephanie had just come in from the kitchen and almost spilled the coffee. "A fake?" she gasped. "That can't be."

"I'm afraid so," said John. "The design is late Victorian. Genuine pieces are worth over fifty thousand. But a lot of paste copies were made."

"A jeweler told us it was real," Gwen protested.

The three cousins stared at each other, crestfallen and embarrassed. "At least we won't be fighting over it," Carol said with a forced little laugh.

John Bitterman stayed and drank his coffee, explaining the ins and outs of costume jewelry, but no one was paying attention. Young Jonah picked up the cold, worthless brooch from the table and examined it. It did look kind of fake, he had to admit. "Mom?"

Carol recognized the tone in his voice. "What's the matter?" she said, crossing to his side.

"I think I know what happened," Jonah whispered.

WHAT DOES JONAH THINK HAPPENED?
WHAT FACT CLUED HIM IN?

TURN TO PAGE 82 FOR THE SOLUTION TO "AUNT PENNY'S BROOCH."

THE DISABLED LOOKOUT

FOR HALF HIS LIFE, Jonah Bixby had been doing his homework in police stations. He would walk to the precinct house right after school, say hello to Sergeant Brown at the front desk, then make his way to some unused room and keep himself busy until his mother got off duty.

One day in late October, Jonah sat alone in an observation room, working on some boring math problems. There was a one-way mirror between him and the interrogation room, and when the lights went on and people started entering the interrogation room, Jonah flipped the microphone switch. He knew he shouldn't do it, but he couldn't resist. It was just like having his own private police reality show.

Jonah was surprised to see his mother beyond the one-way mirror. She was talking to another officer, and Jonah was able to piece together the details of their current case. There had been a robbery that afternoon at a warehouse. The police were tipped off by a silent alarm, but when they arrived on the scene the perpetrators had escaped.

"They obviously had a lookout who warned them," Detective Carol Bixby told her partner. "The area around the warehouse is pretty deserted, but we did manage to round up three suspicious characters. I think we should question them together."

Jonah knew this was unusual. The police almost always preferred to question suspects separately. But when the three men walked into the interrogation room, he saw that this was a highly unusual situation.

The first suspect wore sunglasses and walked with a white cane. He was blind. The second was accompanied by a civilian police employee. They signed back and forth with their hands, and Jonah quickly deduced that this suspect was deaf. The third had his right arm in a plaster cast.

"I guess you should all introduce yourselves," said Detective Bixby. Then she stepped back and watched the almost comical scene as the deaf man signed his "hellos" to his interpreter who spoke them aloud. Then the injured man held out his left hand instead of his right and the deaf man shook it, and the blind man held out his own left in a different direction, trying to find the injured man's hand, and finally... Finally, all the men had exchanged names and greetings.

The deaf man was the first to speak, although his hands did all the talking. He had been on the corner of Spruce and Industry, waiting for a bus. He had seen the police cars driving by. Their lights were flashing, but of course he had no way of knowing if their sirens were on. "I certainly didn't call and warn anyone. How could I?"

The injured man had just come out of his doctor's office when he was picked up. "I broke my arm this morning and just had the cast put on." Carol Bixby felt the plaster and could tell it was still wet.

The blind man said he'd been on his way to a seeing-eye dog facility in the area. "My last dog died two weeks ago," he told the officers. "I can get around without a dog, but it's not easy." He claimed he heard the sirens passing by, but had no idea if they were police or fire trucks or ambulances.

"We'll check out their stories," Carol told her partner. "But we have no cause to hold any of them right now." As she said this, she was standing by the mirror and could hear a light rapping on the glass. It was a code, Jonah's secret code, and Carol Bixby instantly knew her son was on the other side.

"Excuse me," she said to her partner and the suspects. "I'll be right back."

WHICH SUSPECT WAS THE LOOKOUT?
WHAT CLUE DID JONAH CATCH?

TURN TO PAGE 82 FOR THE SOLUTION TO "THE DISABLED LOOKOUT."

JONAH'S NIGHTMARE

JONAH CAME DOWN for breakfast one morning looking tired and worried. "Did you hear a gunshot last night?"

"Gunshot?" His mother stopped pouring cereal into a bowl. "Around here?" Carol Bixby and her son lived on a cul-de-sac with only one other house nearby.

Jonah nodded. "I heard Mr. and Mrs. Grover next door fighting, and then I heard a gunshot. I was so tired, I just went back to sleep, but I'm sure it was a gun."

"You were dreaming," his mother said. "I didn't hear anything."

"Your bedroom's on the other side of the house," Jonah replied. "And you're a sound sleeper. Can we go next door and check it out?"

Carol smiled. "You think the Grovers killed each other? Jonah, you spend too much time with me at work. Not everything is a crime."

But Jonah insisted and Carol knew that the only way to shut him up was to give in. So they both put on jackets and walked across to their neighbors' split-level home. On the front lawn was a "Sold" sign. After months of trying, the Grovers had sold their house just yesterday and were moving to Sacramento, California.

Jonah was about to knock when he heard a banging sound coming from inside. "You see?" he said. Without even thinking, he turned the knob and pushed open the door.

Mr. Grover was alone in the living room, pounding a nail into the wall. "Carol? Jonah?" he said, surprised. "Just a second." And he took a picture from the floor and hung it on the nail. "Come on in," he said, turning to greet them.

Carol blushed. "Sorry to disturb you, Bob, but Jonah thinks he heard something last night. Were you and Dora…" She didn't know quite how to say it. "Were you guys arguing last night?"

"Arguing?" Bob Grover looked puzzled. "No. Dora left yesterday to close on the house in Sacramento. The new owners of this place are coming by any minute for a final walk-through."

"Do you mind if I have a look around?" Jonah asked. "I mean, I don't think I've ever seen your whole house."

Mr. Grover smiled. "The movers are coming Monday to pack us up, so the place is a mess. But sure, knock yourself out."

Carol and Mr. Grover stayed in the living room chatting, while Jonah disappeared into the back rooms. He didn't know what he was looking for, perhaps some evidence of foul play.

The master bedroom looked rumpled and ordinary. Had Mrs. Grover really left yesterday? Jonah checked a closet and saw three suitcases piled high on a shelf. In the master bathroom were the usual cosmetics and toiletries around the sink, but no evidence to suggest Dora hadn't gone away for a few days. He wished he was a trained detective like his mother.

Jonah returned to the living room and finally remembered something. "Mr. Grover?" he said. "Wasn't there a rug in this room?"

"Very observant," said Bob Grover. "Yeah, it was too big for our new house, so Dora gave it to her niece across town."

A minute later, Carol and her son were walking back home. "Well, that was embarrassing," she muttered.

But Jonah wasn't embarrassed, he had just realized. "Mom, you need to call a judge and get a search warrant."

"What?"

"Mr. Grover shot his wife in that house. If we wait too long, he'll get rid of the evidence."

WHAT CONVINCED JONAH THAT
MR. GROVER SHOT HIS WIFE?

TURN TO PAGE 83 FOR THE SOLUTION TO "JONAH'S NIGHTMARE."

THE FBI AND THE HACKER

AS ONE OF THE CITY'S only female detectives, Carol Bixby was often stuck with non-detective chores, like doing paperwork. But it was because she was stuck here at the station house on one particular morning, writing up a boring report, that she was picked to join the FBI on an emergency operation.

The FBI's Computer Fraud Division was on the trail of a hacker who was releasing computer viruses through the Beaverton College e-mail system. The hacker had stayed one step ahead of them, changing computers with every attack. But now they were getting close. Carol helped them get a search warrant and accompanied the FBI agents when they knocked on an apartment door just off campus.

A short young man answered their knock. His name was Oscar Paterno, and he shared the place with two other students. "I know next to nothing about computers," Oscar told them. "When I need one, I go to the school's computer lab."

One of his roommates was there to support this claim. "Yeah, as far as I know, Oscar doesn't even have e-mail," said Mark Gilley. The lanky Australian was in the kitchen, a skillet in his left hand, flipping pancakes. "You blokes want some griddle cakes?" he asked. Carol and the agents declined.

"And where is your computer?" Carol asked the Aussie.

"It died last week," Mark told them. "I'm waiting on a check from Mum and Dad to buy a new one."

The FBI found only one computer in the apartment, a desktop owned by the missing roommate, Boris Brinsky, a math major and chess wizard. They took photos of Boris's room and then packed up the computer for further examination at the lab.

They were just carting it out the door when Boris walked in. "What are you people doing?" he demanded. Carol showed him the search warrant and took him aside to answer questions.

"We traced the hacker to your computer," she told him. "The last virus was sent out at 7:06 this morning."

"It wasn't me. I was in the library all night," Boris said. "I fell asleep in a study cubicle and woke up maybe fifteen minutes ago."

Boris knew of no one who could verify his alibi. And his roommates weren't very helpful either. Both claimed to have been in bed by midnight and not left their rooms until about eight this morning. According to this timetable, any one of them, Boris included, could have sneaked into his room and fired off the code that was once again crippling the college system.

Boris was indignant and refused to sign the Inventory of Confiscation. "What am I going to do without my computer?"

"We don't need your permission," Carol explained. "It's just a formality." She held out the pen until Oscar reached out his right hand and signed for his roommate.

That evening, Carol brought the FBI report home to

study. "Looks like you've got homework, too," Jonah joked when she laid it all out on the kitchen table.

Carol laughed. "Well, I often help you with yours. Maybe you can help with mine. It would be a real coup if I could beat the FBI on this one."

She showed Jonah a photo of Boris's computer before it was moved. It was a new Dell machine, fairly powerful. To the right of the keyboard were a colorful mouse pad and a small stack of yesterday's mail. To the left were a coffee stain, the mouse, and a small desk clock.

"Tell me everything that happened," the twelve-year-old said. "I think I can find your hacker."

WHOM DOES JONAH SUSPECT?
WHAT EVIDENCE POINTS TO THE HACKER?
TURN TO PAGE 83 FOR THE SOLUTION TO "THE FBI AND THE HACKER."

THE LOCKED COTTAGE

"WATCH OUT FOR THE POISON ivy," Jonah shouted, pointing to the shiny, purple-tinged leaves along the side of the cottage.

The man from Central Indiana Power & Gas glanced down at the dangerous weeds, then grabbed a pair of work gloves from his tool belt. "Thanks," he shouted back. With the gloves on, he reached through the leaves to the main valve. "It's all off," he called to Detective Bixby, as he turned the knob all the way. "You can go in."

Just fifteen minutes earlier, a postal carrier had smelled gas coming through the mail slot of Anna Plinkov's little stone cottage. He immediately called the gas company and the police. Carol Bixby had been four blocks away, driving her son to his Saturday baseball practice, and responded to the call.

"All the doors and windows are locked from the inside," Carol observed. She had a rock in her hand and now used it to smash a window by the front door. Reaching inside, she unlatched it. "You stay out here," she warned Jonah, then climbed in through the window. Jonah watched from the porch as one by one the doors and windows of the cottage flew open, letting the poisonous gas escape.

Jonah was still on the front porch when a small sedan pulled up to the curb. A young woman, about 25 years old, sprang out and came toward him, fumbling through a key chain. She stopped as she saw the open door and Jonah standing beside it. "The police called me," she said. "I'm Miss Plinkov's niece. Is there something wrong?" Then she smelled the gas. "Oh, dear." A second later she was running into the house. "Aunt Anna?"

It was five minutes later when a second car pulled up. The driver was a young man, about the same age as the niece. He, too, climbed up the porch steps, smelled the gas, and asked about his aunt.

"I don't know if anyone was home." Jonah tried to sound optimistic. "Maybe the house was empty."

"Aunt Anna is always home." The nephew scratched nervously at a rash on his forearms. "Excuse me, kid," he said, and disappeared into the cottage.

Jonah checked his watch—he was already late for baseball practice—then settled down on the steps. A little while later, his mother came out and sat down beside him. "Bad news." Her face was solemn. "I found the old lady in front of a gas fireplace, one of the kind that you need to light. Last night she settled in with her usual cup of cocoa and a book. She must have turned on the gas and forgotten to light it. Or else the fire blew out."

"Are her lips purple?" Jonah asked, trying to envision the scene.

"Yes," Carol said. "Dead from asphyxiation. Her niece and nephew say they visit her now and then. They say her routine is always the same. An early dinner. Then she locks up the house, lights the fire, and sits down with her cocoa. It looks like a simple accident, except…"

"Except what?"

"Well, Ms. Plinkov had a lot of money in the bank. She had no children and that niece and nephew are her only heirs."

"You should have the lab analyze her cup of cocoa," suggested Jonah. "Maybe one of them put sleeping pills in it."

"That occurred to me, too," Carol said. "But even if they did… The house was locked from the inside. Bolts on the doors; latches on the windows. Miss Plinkov was alive and well when she locked up last night."

Jonah sat and thought. He wanted it to be an accident. Then he could finally get to baseball practice. "Mom," he said reluctantly. "I know how one of them could have killed her."

HOW COULD THE MURDER HAVE BEEN COMMITTED? WHOM DOES JONAH SUSPECT?

TURN TO PAGE 83 FOR THE SOLUTION TO "THE LOCKED COTTAGE."

THE VAMPIRE ON THE BALCONY

THE WITCH AND the young Sherlock Holmes had just left their car in a parking lot and were making their way along Center Street toward the Detective Division's annual Halloween party.

"What if there's a homicide tonight?" Jonah asked with a chuckle. "Are the detectives all going to show up in costume?"

Carol whacked her son playfully with her broomstick. "That's right. Napoleon and Frankenstein will be on the case. And Sherlock Holmes, of course."

It was October 31, and a festive assortment of ghouls and ghosts strolled up and down the street. Adding to the spirit were the decorations—paper skeletons stapled to doors, comical tombstones. Jonah and his mother took a shortcut down a side alley on their way to the party. Jonah saw that someone on the third floor had placed a Dracula dummy in a chair on a balcony, with a stake through its heart.

"Mom," Jonah said, tugging on her sleeve. His face was suddenly ashen. "That's not a stake—it's a corkscrew. And that's not a dummy. It's a real man."

As they looked on, the door opened and a zombie and a gypsy woman stepped out onto the balcony. The gypsy woman smiled and touched the corpse on the shoulder, then took a closer look at the corkscrew. Her scream was piercing.

"Looks like we'll have to skip our own party," Detective Bixby told her son. "I don't even have time to take you home."

"That's okay," said Jonah, trying to act as though he didn't care. The only thing better than a Halloween party, in his mind, was a Halloween party with a real crime to solve.

His mother brought him up to the third-floor apartment, and they walked in on twenty costumed guests, all looking shocked and ready to leave. When the other officers arrived, Carol instructed them to take statements.

During all of this, Jonah was pretty much ignored. He glanced around at the new furniture, then wandered into the kitchen and saw the spanking-new appliances and cookware, one of everything. "This is what they call a corporate apartment," his mother explained as she passed by. "All very basic."

The victim was a businessman from New York, Thad Jericho, who used the apartment about once a week. He had been hosting this Halloween party for his local employees when one of them must have joined him on the balcony and stabbed him to death.

The zombie they'd seen on the balcony approached Detective Bixby. "I'm Kendall Brown, office manager," he said, wiping a dribble of fake blood from his mouth.

Carol Bixby nodded. "From the statements we've been getting, it seems Mr. Jericho wasn't very popular."

The zombie shrugged. "He made a lot of unpopular decisions. And to make it worse, Thad was a bit of a jerk…"

"A big jerk," said a newcomer. It was the gypsy woman, otherwise known as Gina Morrissey, personnel director.

"Did anyone see Mr. Jericho go out on the balcony?" Carol asked.

"No," said Kendall. "No one remembers seeing him for at least half an hour before the body was discovered."

"Actually, I think I discovered the body," said a cowboy who had just joined them. His name was Herbert Horner, senior accountant. "I got here rather late."

"Right," Gina agreed. "We didn't think you were coming. I was just uncorking the last bottle of wine when you walked in."

"That's not my point," said Herbert. "My point is I took a shortcut through the alley. I saw Thad up on the balcony, already dead. I thought it was just a decoration."

"Did you see anything else?" Carol asked.

"No," said Herbert. "I just came up and joined the party. About ten minutes later, Gina and Kendall found him out there."

"Mom," Jonah whispered. "I need to talk to you."

For the first time, the guests noticed that there was a twelve-year-old among them dressed as Sherlock Holmes. Gina cracked a smug smile. "Looks like we have our own little detective here. Maybe you can tell us who killed him."

Jonah looked up to his mother. "Can I, Mom?"

"Go ahead," Carol said and saw the gypsy's smile fade.

WHO KILLED THAD JERICHO?
WHAT CLUE DID JONAH NOTICE?

TURN TO PAGE 84 FOR THE SOLUTION TO "VAMPIRE ON THE BALCONY."

A TEST FOR ROOKIES

THE ART GALLERY OWNER sat in a folding chair in the interview room. He looked bruised and nervous as Detective Carol Bixby sat across from him and listened to his story.

"I just closed up the gallery for the night," he told her. "We had a lot of cash in the register, very unusual for us. I wanted to get the money to the bank as soon as possible."

"So you drove over to Beaverton Federal Bank," Detective Bixby prodded.

"That's right," the gallery owner confirmed. "They have a walk-up night depository."

"Did you notice that you were being followed?"

"No. Not until the other car pulled up and the guy got out. He was wearing a ski mask. I tried to get back in my car, but he was too fast. He pulled a knife, like a hunting knife, and demanded the deposit bag."

"You shouldn't have resisted," Carol said. "You could have been killed."

The owner winced and nodded. "I guess it was just instinct. I swung the bag at him. But somehow he managed to stab me." He pointed to his right thigh. His pants were torn in a bloody slit, and under the slit was a flesh wound, perfectly centered with the slashed fabric.

"Anyway," he continued, "I fell down screaming with pain. The guy took the bag and ran off."

"What did you do then?" Carol asked.

"I got to my car and grabbed a towel from the floor." He pointed to a hand towel, folded neatly in quarters, with a splotch of blood covering the right half. "Then I called 911 on my cell phone. Look, can I go to the hospital now and get this wound looked at?"

"No, I don't think so," Carol said and smiled.

The art gallery owner, otherwise known as Detective Peter Pauling, smiled back, then stood up and faced the one-way mirror. "All right, rookies. You've just seen an interview with yours truly as a robbery victim. What's your first impression?"

In the observation room on the other side of the glass, four rookie detectives sat in chairs, taking notes. Detectives Pauling and Bixby had found that this kind of class was the best way to teach observation techniques.

"You lied," said one rookie. "You robbed your own store."

"Good," Detective Pauling said. "And what makes you say that?"

A second rookie raised his hand, before realizing they couldn't see him. "The towel, sir. If you'd taken it from your car, it wouldn't have been neatly folded. You obviously prepped the towel, getting it ready before stabbing yourself in the leg."

"Excellent," said Carol Bixby to the mirror. "Anything else?"

The third rookie spoke up. "It's a big coincidence, saying this robbery occurred on the same day as a big cash deposit. Also, it seems kind of odd getting stabbed in the leg like that."

"Also, there were no other witnesses," said the fourth.

"That's good, but it's circumstantial. Anything more concrete?" There was nothing but silence from the four rookies.

"Come on, guys," said Carol impatiently. "I have a twelve-year-old son who's more observant than that. Jonah!" she called out. "I'm sure you saw it. Why don't you tell these officers what they missed?"

The four rookies turned and for the first time noticed a twelve-year-old boy sitting in the rear of the observation room in the shadows.

WHAT CLUE DID THE ROOKIES MISS?

TURN TO PAGE 84 FOR THE SOLUTION TO "A TEST FOR ROOKIES."

DEATH AT THE DOOR

DETECTIVE CAROL BIXBY did her best not to bring Jonah to murder scenes. But sometimes it couldn't be avoided, like today. They had been at the mall, happily buying supplies for the new school year, when the call came in. Judge Roberta Morton had been found shot to death in her home.

"This is really bad," Carol kept repeating as she raced out to the murder scene, screeching around corners with a red, flashing bubble attached to her car roof.

Jonah found himself belted into the passenger seat, along for the furious ride. "Why is it bad?" he asked.

"Judge Morton had been receiving anonymous death threats. She was under police protection until today."

"And she gets killed the same day?" Jonah whistled. "Wow. That is bad."

Jonah and his mother arrived at the secluded country house and entered through a side door. A crime-scene team was already on the premises, along with Carol's partner, Detective Peter Pauling. He said hello to them both and quickly brought them up to speed.

"Dr. Morton was the last person to see his wife alive." They eyed a tall, angular man in hospital scrubs sitting on a sofa, his head buried in his hands. "This morning, he says, was like any other morning." Pauling looked over his notes. "Morton is a surgeon. He's up at six every day and out of the house by 6:30. Judge Morton gets up around seven. She makes coffee and then sits down and watches the morning news."

Carol Bixby crossed to the television. It was still on, and a technician was dusting it and nearly everything else for prints. There were slippers in front of a comfortable-looking chair and a cup of cold coffee on an end table.

"Did anyone hear the shot?" Carol asked.

"No," said Detective Pauling. "We're guessing the time of death was around 7:30, after she made coffee and before she got dressed for work." He pointed around the living room, re-creating the scene. "The judge is watching the news and traffic, just waking up, when the doorbell rings. She opens the door and bang—shot twice in the chest."

Carol and Jonah wandered over to the entry hall, now cordoned off with yellow tape. The body had been removed, but red slashes of blood still decorated the walls and floor. "How far did the shooter get into the house?" Carol asked the technician.

"Don't know," he answered. "There was no reason for him to go inside, but we're dusting and taking samples just in case."

The body had been discovered around noon by the mail carrier. "He's still here," Detective Pauling told his partner. "You want to speak with him?"

Carol and her son found the mailman standing beside his USPS truck, taking nervous drags from a cigarette. "Her car was in the driveway when I got here," he stammered. "That was strange, but I thought maybe she was sick or taking the day off. Then I saw the front door open and something lying in the hall." He shivered. "I didn't touch a thing, honest. I just called the cops."

A technician was just leaving the house and stopped to give a preliminary report. "We found a lot of prints we assume are from Judge and Dr. Morton. A few places were wiped clean—the bell and the doorknob, as you might expect. Also the coffeemaker and the TV remote. We'll know more by tomorrow."

Detective Bixby was heading back into the house when she turned. Jonah wasn't following her. He was just standing on the front lawn, thinking. "What's the matter?" she asked. "Don't tell me you know who killed her?"

"Okay, I won't," said Jonah, but it was clear that he did.

WHO KILLED JUDGE ROBERTA MORTON?
WHAT CLUE POINTS TO THE KILLER?

TURN TO PAGE 85 FOR THE SOLUTION TO "DEATH AT THE DOOR."

FRANKIE AND THE TELESCOPE

IT WAS EARLY AUGUST, one of the worst days of the heat wave, as Jonah and Sally Smith stood in the sweltering tree house in the Smiths' backyard. They were staring at the spot by the window where the rusty telescope used to be. "Someone stole it," Sally repeated for the third time. "My little brother said he saw someone out here this morning. Some kid."

"That makes sense," Jonah said. He couldn't imagine a grown-up making off with the cumbersome old telescope. The detective's son examined the tree house for a minute or so, then climbed down and inspected the ground around the tree.

"You think we should call the police?" asked Sally.

"Why don't we investigate this on our own?" Jonah suggested. He knew the police wouldn't pay much attention to a battered old telescope taken from an unlocked tree house. "It was one person," he quickly deduced, pointing to footsteps in the dirt. "The thief dragged it over here and lifted it over your back fence."

Sally bent down and saw the line in the dirt where the large telescope had been dragged along. On the top edge of the fence was a scratch of black paint and scuff marks from a pair of shoes. Beyond the fence was a vacant lot covered in waist-high weeds.

"He left a path," Jonah said, pointing to the trampled trail curving through the lot. "Come on. Let's follow it."

He started to climb the fence, but Sally stopped him. "No. That lot is full of hornet nests. I got stung there last week—a huge, red, itchy welt."

"Thanks for the warning," Jonah said, studying the trampled trail from a distance. "The telescope was dragged through to Juniper Street. We'll go around."

They grabbed their bikes and raced each other to Juniper, screeching to a halt where the trampled weeds met the sidewalk. "He went this way," Jonah said, following the almost imperceptible scratches in the cement. And then the tracks stopped.

"I guess he carried it from here," Jonah said, a little disappointed. He stood in the middle of the street and looked at the surrounding houses. "Frankie Rooter lives right there," he said, pointing to a two-story house.

"Frankie?" said Sally. "Didn't he steal that baseball from Crazy Kate's shack?" Before Jonah could answer, Sally was crossing the street. He had never seen her so mad. "Frankie?" she shouted toward a figure visible in a second-story window. "Give me back my telescope."

Jonah could see a kid in the room. It was Frankie, all right. He had already heard Sally and was hurrying to open the window.

"What are you doing?" he shouted down at Sally. "You're crazy."

"You stole the telescope from my tree house."

"I did not. I've been in the house all day."

"That's not what Jonah says," Sally countered. "And he's a detective."

"Hey, I didn't say it was Frankie," Jonah protested. "All I said…" But it was too late. He could already hear Frankie rushing down the stairs.

The Rooters' front door flew open, and Frankie emerged, putting on a light jacket as he stepped outside. "All right, Bixby, I'm sick and tired of you calling me a thief."

"Well, you did steal that baseball," Jonah hemmed.

"Hey, I gave it back," he said, going nose to nose with Jonah. "As for your precious telescope, I didn't take it. You want to call me a liar?"

Jonah swallowed hard. And then the answer came. "Yeah, Frankie, I think I do."

HOW DOES JONAH KNOW FRANKIE IS LYING?

TURN TO PAGE 86 FOR THE SOLUTION TO "FRANKIE AND THE TELESCOPE."

A SUICIDAL MURDER

DETECTIVE BIXBY SIGHED and looked across to her son. "You like impossible crimes. Why don't you take a look at this?"

Jonah and his mother were sitting across from each other at the kitchen table, both of them working on their homework for the evening. In Carol Bixby's case, the homework was a homicide investigation.

"Sure." Jonah liked any kind of crime, especially if it meant putting aside an English class assignment. "What kind of impossible crime?" He got up and walked around to look at the police reports spread out on the table.

"A murder made to look like suicide." And she began to outline the case.

Simon Wentworth had been found on the street in front of the building where he lived. It seemed that the young man used a screwdriver to remove the child safety bars from a window in his high-rise apartment. Then he jumped to his death.

Among the photos was a picture of another window with the safety bars still attached to the outside of the building. "Looks like the bars would be tricky to remove," Jonah observed.

"They're supposed to be hard to remove," said Carol. "Anyway, his prints were on the screwdriver and a suicide note was found in his room. No one else had been at home, according to the doorman. And his friends testified that he'd been moody and distracted lately. It's got all the markings of a suicide. Except..." She sighed.

"We interviewed one his neighbors," Carol continued. "Simon shouted, 'No, no, no,' before he jumped—and he screamed all the way down."

"That doesn't sound like suicide," Jonah agreed.

Carol nodded. "It turns out Simon lived in the apartment with his older brother Teddy. We found a partial print of Teddy's on the same screwdriver. So we had Simon's suicide note analyzed by an expert and found a lot of similarities with Teddy's handwriting. To cap it off, it seems the brothers had just taken out million-dollar insurance policies on each other's life."

Jonah picked up a photocopy of the suicide note. It was short and sweet: "I can't go on with the pain anymore. Forgive me, little brother. You'll be better off without me." He examined the penmanship and saw that it did look a little unnatural, with several fits and starts.

"What did Teddy say about his brother's death?" Jonah asked.

"A cool customer," said Carol, shaking her head. "He pretended to be distraught. He was the first to suggest that Simon's death might be murder."

"Let me guess," Jonah said. "Teddy Wentworth has an alibi."

"A great alibi. At the time Simon fell, Teddy was at his

office, on the phone to a client in Los Angeles."

"Maybe he was using a cell phone," Jonah suggested.

"No," said Carol, holding up a sheet of phone records. "He was on his land line at the office. And don't forget the apartment doorman. He says Teddy didn't come in or out the building all during that time."

"Good puzzle," said Jonah. He stood over the table full of papers and scanned them one by one.

"It's not a puzzle," Carol chided. "It's serious. If we don't figure this out, a killer is going to go free."

"Well, I think I know what happened," Jonah said slowly. "But you're not going to like it."

WHAT DOES JONAH THINK HAPPENED?

TURN TO PAGE 86 FOR THE SOLUTION TO "A SUICIDAL MURDER."

ONE DROP OF BLOOD

"PLEASE, MOM, MAY I go? I'll be careful."

Jonah had been sitting at an empty desk in the police department bullpen doing his homework and feeling bored. And then Fred Coombs of the Crime Scene Unit volunteered to take him on a short field trip.

"I don't like you being at homicide scenes," Carol Bixby told her son.

"Come on," said Fred. "It's the cleanest homicide scene in the world. In fact, that's our problem. We can't find a fingerprint or a drop of blood." There was a pleading look on Fred's face. Carol knew how desperately he wanted to borrow her genius son to help him out.

She sighed and gave in. "Okay. Just this once."

Thirty minutes later and Fred was leading the twelve-year-old into a bright, sunlit artist's studio in an industrial building across town. As they put on their plastic gloves, Fred explained the situation.

"A young model is missing. Gina Washington. She was last seen walking into this building. She was coming here to visit Chester Hart, her ex-boyfriend. He's a well-known artist. That was Tuesday around noon. A security video shows Chester two hours later carrying a rolled-up rug out of the building."

"Wow. You think Ms. Washington's body was in the rug?" asked Jonah, cringing at the thought.

"We do," said Fred. "Chester returned that night with two buckets full of cleaning supplies. The security video shows him leaving the building three hours later. We think he killed her here in his studio. He came back to clean the place and did a great job. All we need is one of Gina's fingerprints or a hair or a drop of her blood. Without that, we don't have a case."

"What did Mr. Hart say happened?"

"He says he never saw her that day. He says she must have come into this building to visit someone else. Likely story."

The loft was a large, bright room with a small bathroom off to one side. There were various easels and unfinished paintings propped up against the walls. Everything else was spotless and white, from the light fixtures to the sliding dimmer switch to the bright, gauzy curtains.

"Were the curtains open like that when you got here?" Jonah asked.

"We didn't change a thing," said the crime scene technician. "The curtains were open and the lights were on. As you can see, there are no neighbors with a view of this window."

Jonah nodded. "If he brought two buckets of cleaning supplies, there must have been a lot to clean up."

"Well, he was thorough. No DNA, not a hair or fingerprint to place Gina here. We keep thinking he must have missed a spot, but..."

"I can think of one thing," Jonah said, almost casually.

"Holy..." Fred couldn't help himself. "I guess they're right about you. I didn't really believe it, but..."

"There is one thing he probably changed in this room between the time he killed her and the time he cleaned up. Maybe, just maybe, he forgot to clean there."

Fred clapped his hands. "All right, let's check it out."

WHERE DOES JONAH THINK THERE MIGHT BE A SPOT OF EVIDENCE?

TURN TO PAGE 87 FOR THE SOLUTION TO "ONE DROP OF BLOOD."

THE SECRET LETTERS

"MOM, PLEASE, I want to go," Jonah insisted. "We must have something up here that's old and interesting."

Jonah and his mother were in the attic, searching through the piles of clothes and knickknacks and discarded furniture. Carol Bixby sighed as she dusted away a layer of cobwebs. "I don't think Traveling Treasures is going to be interested in your father's moldy neckties," she said, moving aside a box.

"How about these bookends?" Jonah held up a pair of small iron roosters. "They're old and ugly, so they must be valuable." He dusted them off. "What do you say?"

Every Sunday night, Jonah and his mother sat down and watched Traveling Treasures, where hundreds of people brought in their family heirlooms and had them appraised by a platoon of experts. This week, the TV show was filming in Indianapolis, just an hour's drive away. From the minute Jonah saw the announcement on the news, he'd been bugging his mother to go.

"All right," Carol conceded. "It'll be a nice day trip. But you can't be disappointed."

Jonah promised. He really just wanted to do it for the fun and the experience. But by Saturday afternoon, after driving to the Convention Center and waiting in four different lines, it was a major letdown when an antiques dealer from New York evaluated his rooster bookends. The pieces were late Victorian, mass-produced, and worth about ten dollars each.

"There weren't even any cameras around," Jonah sulked.

"They save the cameras for the good stuff," Carol said with a smile. "Come on. Let's see who got lucky."

For the rest of the day, they wandered the hall, looking on as the resident experts appraised everything from baseball cards to gold chandeliers. Carol and Jonah were just approaching the exit when one particular item caught Carol's eye. "Oh, look," she said. "There's a terrific desk. Let's see what it's worth."

They stopped and watched as the furniture expert spoke to the desk's owner, a young woman. "It's an Edwardian piece," he explained somewhat pompously. "Made in England. Fairly common." He ran a hand under the front of the huge wooden desk. "I think it has a hidden drawer."

"Really?" the young owner said. "The desk belonged to my great grandmother, and I never..."

She stopped in mid-sentence, surprised, as the appraiser lifted a small section of molding and a secret drawer eased open. He reached deep inside and pulled out what looked like a steel cigar box, secured with a rusty clasp.

"Oh, my," the desk's owner said. "It must have been in there forever and no one knew."

Up until this moment, the expert had been looking bored. Now he was beginning to get excited. "Do you mind if I open it?" Without even waiting for an answer, he gently turned the clasp and lifted the box's tight-fitting lid.

Jonah and his mother had a good view. Inside the small

steel box, under a layer of dust, they saw a stack of letters tied with a red ribbon. "Love letters?" the expert joked. "Was your great grandmother involved in some secret romance?"

"Well…" The young woman seemed a little sheepish. "There is a family story that before she married my great grandfather, she was friends with the young Winston Churchill, but…"

Even as she said it, the expert was holding the pack of letters under a light and squinting at a handwritten signature. He gasped and nearly choked on the dust. Seconds later, he was squawking into his cell phone. "Get a camera crew over here. Station 16. We're going to need a documents expert, too. This is big."

"Love letters from Churchill," whispered Carol. "Wow. Can you believe it?"

"No, I can't," said Jonah. "It's a fake."

"What do you mean, fake?"

"I mean that woman planted the letters in that box and tried to make them look old. I'll bet you anything they're forgeries."

HOW DID JONAH KNOW THE LETTERS WERE PLANTED?

TURN TO PAGE 87 FOR THE SOLUTION TO "THE SECRET LETTERS."

UNDERCOVER JONAH

"MOM, I LOOK LIKE a stupid penguin."

Jonah waddled back and forth in front of the museum, pretending to be outraged by the rented tuxedo. In reality, though, Jonah thought it was kind of cool being dressed up like James Bond and taking part in his first undercover assignment.

"Jonah, stop," Carol Bixby hissed as she straightened the straps of her formal gown. "The first rule is not to draw attention to yourself."

"Sorry." Jonah didn't blame his mother for being upset. After all, she and the other police detectives had worked long hours to ensure that tonight's event ran smoothly.

The event was a charity gala featuring five newly acquired sculptures. They were modern pieces and each statue was accented in real fur. That was why the museum needed such security. Anti-fur protestors were picketing the museum, and some had even threatened to crash the gala and destroy the offending works of art.

At the front of the line, Jonah handed the guard his long rectangular ticket and got in return the ticket's torn square stub. Then he and his mother stepped through metal detectors and underwent a bag search. Once inside the grand lobby, they blended in with the other formally dressed guests, except that Detective Carol Bixby wore an earpiece and had a police-issue handgun in her fancy little purse.

The crowd was just beginning to wander back toward the exhibition rooms when her earpiece began to squawk. "Silent alarm," a voice informed her. "Exhibition Hall J."

"The statue room," Carol whispered to her son and started sprinting in that direction. Jonah followed and so did two other undercover "guests." All four of them wound their way through the labyrinth of hallways and arrived at about the same moment, rushing into Exhibition Hall J and finding it freshly vandalized.

Jonah saw the five statues in the center of the room, each one with a red "X" sprayed across it. On one of the walls was a message, also in red paint. "Fur Is Mur..." it said, the last letter trailing off into nothing.

Carol Bixby scanned the room, then pointed to a window high in the wall. The glass had been shattered, and footprints on the marble floor showed where the intruder had jumped down into the room of statues. Near the doorway was the abandoned can of spray paint and a pair of plastic gloves.

"How did he get out?" one of the plainclothes officers asked.

"He didn't," Carol said. "It's been less than a minute since the broken window triggered the alarm. He barely had enough time to jump to the floor, do his damage with the paint, and run off. He must still be in the museum."

A sudden flash of cameras alerted them to the photographers gathered around. The reporters who were there to document the gala opening now had a bigger story on their hands. The vandals had won, Jonah thought. They had gotten their publicity.

Half an hour later, Carol Bixby and her son were in the museum office, interviewing witnesses.

The first was the city Councilman Grover Prescott, who had been a vocal opponent of the fur exhibition. He was in a dark brown suit, one of the only guests not in formal wear. "Right after I got through security, I went to use the bathroom," the councilman told Carol. "I was just coming out when I saw this man run by. A young guy in a tuxedo, that's all I could see. A couple seconds later, you and your people came running from the other direction."

The second witness was Rhett Aronson, a young animal-rights activist. "And just what are you doing here?" Carol demanded.

"I have a right," Rhett protested, taking from his pocket the same long rectangular ticket that everyone else had used to gain admission. Jonah looked at the man's feet and saw that he was wearing black fabric shoes and not the typical patent-leather tuxedo shoes.

The interview was interrupted by a uniformed officer. "We sealed the doors as soon as we could," he reported to his superior. "He must have already made his escape."

As soon as the officer and the activist walked out, Jonah leaned over to his mother. "The bad guy didn't escape," Jonah whispered. "He's still in the museum."

WHO IS THE SPRAY PAINT VANDAL?
WHAT CLUE DID JONAH NOTICE?

TURN TO PAGE 88 FOR THE SOLUTION TO "UNDERCOVER JONAH."

THE DYING CLUE

DETECTIVE CAROL BIXBY gazed at the corpse and couldn't shake the feeling that she was taking part in a cheesy mystery novel. She had heard stories about murder victims writing a last dying message in their own blood. Such things actually did occur. But why would someone use his last ounce of strength to crawl over to a wall and write in blood...his own name? It made no sense.

The murder scene was in the offices of Martinez and Kramer, certified public accountants. It was an oddly shaped space. In the front was a reception area guarded by Mona Lapinski, a middle-aged assistant. Behind her station, the office split like an Y, with two long corridors angling off. At the end of one corridor was a frosted glass door, with painted letters proclaiming "Douglas Kramer." At the end of the other corridor was a similar frosted door, this one with the name of his partner, "Gil Martinez."

On the day of the murder, Mona left the office around noon to walk in the park and eat the sandwich and apple she brought every day from home. Gil Martinez left a few minutes later to have lunch with a client at his private club. That left Douglas Kramer alone in his office.

Mona was the one to find his body. "I was coming back

from the park," she said in her statement. "I saw Larry, the guy from Worldwide Parcel, on the sidewalk, ringing our buzzer. He said no one was answering, which isn't unusual at lunchtime. I signed for the parcel, said good-bye to Larry, and unlocked the door. People in this building are very good about security. Strangers don't get in."

"Anyway," Mona continued, stopping to take in a deep breath. "The parcel was for Mr. Martinez, so when I got inside, I took it straight back to his office. A soon as I walked in…" She shivered. "Chairs turned over, lamps broken. And the blood."

When Gil Martinez walked in a minute later, he found Mona standing in his private office, screaming at the top of her lungs. His business partner, Douglas Kramer, lay next to the wall, a pair of scissors embedded in his stomach. On the wall, by his outstretched hand, were four letters printed in blood. "D-O-U-G."

"Doug and I weren't really friends," Martinez told the detective. "The last time I saw him was this morning. He came into my office to borrow a pair of scissors." He identified the scissors, which were currently sticking out of his partner's stomach.

Detective Bixby pointed to a brown leather wallet, untainted by the blood, sitting prominently on his bloody desktop. "Mr. Martinez, this is a crime scene. Did you just put that here?"

"No, no," he replied. "I forgot it when I left. I charged my lunch on my account at the club. That wallet's been here all day." Carol put on plastic gloves, then checked the contents— three credit cards and two hundred twenty dollars in cash.

Nothing was missing.

The last interview was with Larry Baker, the delivery guy. He'd been called back by his dispatcher and didn't seem too pleased to have his route interrupted. "I don't know what I can tell you," he said. "I had several deliveries in that building today, but I didn't see anything unusual. I made two trips from my truck. On the second, I ran into their assistant and she signed for the package. I didn't even go inside again."

"Do you make a lot of deliveries to Martinez and Kramer?" Carol asked.

Larry thought for a moment. "Couple times a week. But I never met either one of those guys. I just dealt with the assistant. From the way she talked, I got the sense that they didn't get along."

Carol drove back to the station house. Her shift was almost over, and Jonah was probably there waiting for her. She hated thinking that her twelve-year-old son might be able to solve this puzzle when she couldn't, so she reviewed the case in her mind.

Robbery couldn't be the motive, since Gil Martinez's wallet was still on his desk, untouched. The security camera showed no strangers entering, and everyone else in the building at the time had an alibi. But the big question was why. Why were those four letters scrawled on the wall?

WHO KILLED DOUGLAS KRAMER?
WHY WAS "D-O-U-G" WRITTEN ON THE WALL?
TURN TO PAGE 88 FOR THE SOLUTION TO "THE DYING CLUE."

LEMONADE 25¢

REALTY
FOR
SALE
SOLD

WHO TOOK THE TIP?

IT WAS A WARM SATURDAY afternoon, and Jonah was on his skateboard, negotiating the curvy sidewalk along River Road. That's when he almost hit the lemonade stand. He saw it just in time, swerving, then tumbling onto a brand-new lawn in front of a brand-new house.

"Are you okay?" asked Denny. Denny was Sally Smith's eight-year-old brother. He was the one who'd set up his business right in the middle of the sidewalk.

Jonah brushed himself off. "You need to find a better spot to sell lemonade."

"No way," said Denny, not quite understanding what Jonah meant. "This is the best. See those guys moving furniture?" He pointed to two workmen who were pushing a final sofa up a ramp and into the house. "They bought nineteen glasses."

"Wow." Jonah was impressed and his irritation dissolved.

"Yeah, it's great," said Denny, but his smile dipped at the corners. "There's just one problem."

Then, as if on cue, the problem came riding up on his bike. It was Frankie Rooter. Frankie was a year older than Jonah, big for his age, and fast becoming a real bully.

"Give me another one," Frankie growled at Denny.

"Hey." Jonah stepped forward. "You want lemonade,

Frankie? Pay for it."

"No, that's all right," Denny said. He had already poured a glass and was handing it over. That's when they heard the shouts coming from just inside the new house.

Through the open door, the boys could hear two men arguing at full volume. A second later, one of the men came to the door and saw them on the sidewalk. "You kids. Come in here now." He spoke with such authority that not even Frankie hesitated.

Inside the front door was a spacious entryway, with three corridors branching off in different directions and a grand staircase going up. The man who had ordered them inside was the moving-van driver. The other man was smaller, almost timid-looking. But right now he was angry. They were both angry.

The smaller man introduced himself. He'd just had the house built and was new to the neighborhood. "Were any of you boys in this house today?" he demanded. "Tell me the truth."

All three boys denied it. "I came up to the door once," Denny admitted. "To see if anyone wanted more lemonade. But I didn't go inside."

"I'm telling you," the moving-van driver said, "some kid was in here. I heard him sneaking around. And then I caught a glimpse of him running out the patio door."

"But you don't know which kid it was...?"

The mover looked over all three and shook his head. "No. I didn't really see him. But it was a kid. He's the one who stole the money."

"Stole money?" Jonah gasped. It was a terrible thing to

happen to a new neighbor—and an even worse thing to be accused of.

"I left it on the kitchen counter," the homeowner explained. "In an envelope. It was tip money for the driver and his men."

"Well, I never saw it," the driver said. "Either some kid took it, or you never left it in the first place."

"Go ask your moving guys," said Frankie. He was starting to squirm a little and make faces. "I'll bet one of them took it."

"No way," said the driver. He was about to say something more, but Frankie's squirming distracted him. "Why are you twitching, kid? What's wrong?"

"I have to pee," Frankie moaned. "Too much lemonade."

Both men chuckled, then resumed their discussion. They continued to argue, with the owner refusing to leave another tip and the driver accusing him of trying to cheat them. And while all this happened, Frankie fidgeted.

"Sorry!" Frankie finally shouted and raced down one of the hallways. He opened the first door on the right and ducked into the downstairs bathroom.

As soon as Frankie was gone, Jonah got up enough courage to speak. "Excuse me," he said to the owner, pulling his sleeve and taking him aside. He lowered his voice to a whisper. "You don't know me, sir. But I'm a pretty good detective. And I know what happened to your money."

WHO TOOK THE TIP MONEY?
WHAT CLUE DID JONAH NOTICE?

TURN TO PAGE 89 FOR THE SOLUTION TO "WHO TOOK THE TIP?"

THE BURNING BUNGALOW

"MOM, PLEASE, I'VE NEVER been inside a fire scene," Jonah whined.

"And you're not getting into this one," Carol said flatly. They were standing in front of a small bungalow on Beaverton's north side. The charred walls were still standing, but the fire had been intense enough to kill the home's single resident, a pretty, young waitress named Sarah Simmons who had lived there with her beloved cat. The arson investigator was here to determine if it was an accident or not, while Detective Bixby was on hand to oversee the removal of the body and preserve the scene, in case it proved to be homicide.

Jonah's mother joined the other investigators inside the bungalow, leaving him alone on the porch. "I tried to stop her, but she wouldn't listen," said a choked voice from behind him. Jonah turned to see a nervous little man with a thin, hawklike face. He introduced himself as Billy Borenson, Sarah's neighbor.

"I just came home from the grocery store when I saw the fire." He pointed to his car, parked haphazardly in the driveway of the bungalow next door. "Her house was filled with flames. They were coming out the windows. I'm the one who called 911," he said, rather proudly. "I guess everyone else on the block was at work or something."

Jonah had no reason not to like Billy Borenson, but he didn't need a reason. The guy just seemed creepy. "What do you mean, you tried to stop her?"

"Oh, I mean Sarah. I would have gone in to save her, you know. But she came out just as I was about to. We stood on the lawn together, just waiting for the fire engines. And then I was dumb enough to ask about her cat, Mr. Tibbs. Before I could stop her, Sarah was running back in the house, calling for her cat."

"Why didn't you go in after her?" Jonah asked. He was a little irritated by the man's false boasts of bravery.

"That would've been suicide," Borenson said. "There were flames everywhere, even on the floor…" He stopped as he saw a younger man running up the driveway. "Uh-oh," he whispered to Jonah. "That's Sarah's boyfriend. Ex-boyfriend, I mean."

The man joined them on the porch, looking dazed. "What happened?" he asked, looking through the doorway and into the charred house. "I was here just an hour ago."

"I know," said Billy Borenson. "I could hear you and Sarah fighting from my house."

"What Sarah and I do is none of your business," the boyfriend snapped.

"Maybe," said Borenson. "But you were pretty mad. The firefighters think it might have been started by a cigarette in a trash can." Jonah's head was at about the same height as the boyfriend's chest, and he could easily see a pack of cigarettes stuffed into his shirt pocket.

"Really?" The boyfriend shrugged. "Where's Sarah?"

Neither Borenson nor Jonah had to answer that question, for just a second later two officers emerged through the doorway carrying a black plastic body bag. "Sarah!" the boyfriend shouted and almost dove at the bag.

"Please, sir, step back," said one of the officers. But Sarah's boyfriend stayed with them, calling out her name, all the way to the medical examiner's van.

Jonah looked back into the house. His mother and the arson investigator stood on the blackened remains of the living room rug. Right by their feet was a perfectly preserved piece of green carpet outlining the spot where Sarah's body had been lying.

Jonah wanted to go in and maybe have a look around. But he restrained himself. A few minutes later, Carol Bixby came out. "They think it's arson," she said simply. "So this is a murder scene."

"I know."

Carol recognized that tone of voice. "Okay, Jonah. What exactly do you know?"

WHOM DOES JONAH SUSPECT OF MURDER?
WHAT WAS THE CLUE?

TURN TO PAGE 90 FOR THE SOLUTION TO "THE BURNING BUNGALOW."

SOLUTIONS

SOLUTION TO "THE HAUNTED TREE HOUSE"

Sally pointed at Jonah. "Look, he's laughing. Jonah did it."

"No," Jonah protested between chuckles. "Not me. But I know who. Tell 'em, Lisa."

"Me?" Lisa said. She was scowling, but the scowl erupted into a giggle. "All right, it was me. I took the key last Halloween, just like you said."

"But the key was on the ledge above the window," said Bill.

"Nope," said Lisa. "It was in my hand. I dropped it while I was pretending to brush the ledge. You couldn't tell the difference—except for Jonah."

"No, you were good," Jonah admitted. "I didn't see a thing."

"Then how did you know?"

"Because the key was bright and shiny. Everything else in this place is rusty and moldy. As soon as the key hit the floor, I knew it hadn't spent the winter here."

SOLUTION TO "AFTER-SCHOOL HOMICIDE"

Carol had taken her son into the front showroom. "You are not allowed into murder scenes, young man."

"It's not going to give me nightmares," Jonah said, although he wasn't quite sure about that.

"Good." Then she smiled. "What did you see in there?"

"It's not what I saw—it's what I didn't see. There's no blood in the safe. There's blood on the safe door, but not inside, meaning…"

"Meaning the safe was closed when Mr. Clawson was shot…" Carol rubbed her jaw. "Which brings up the question…"

"Who opened the safe?" Jonah liked it when he and his mother finished each other's sentences. He tried it once more. "The only other person who probably knows the combination is…"

"Clawson's partner, Madelyn Wolfe. So, you're telling me there wasn't any guy in a ski mask?"

Jonah nodded. "I think she killed him, stole the stuff in the safe, then locked herself in the closet. If you check her pockets or some-where nearby, I'll bet you find the closet key."

SOLUTION TO "CRAZY KATE"

"You live right by the park," Frankie said, pointing across the street. "I'll bet some kids were playing baseball and hit one through your window. They broke in to get it back. That's when they found your baseball and swiped it."

"Sounds logical," Crazy Kate had to admit.

"No," said Jonah. "That theory doesn't explain the phone call get-ting you out of your house. No, ma'am, it was Frankie."

"Me?" Frankie was outraged. "You're lying. I got here the same time you did."

"Really?" Jonah asked. "Then why did you walk into her yard and up to her front door without calling out? She could have shot you with birdseed."

"No, she couldn't," Frankie said. "She wasn't home."

"But how did you know she wasn't home?" Frankie didn't have an answer. "You knew because you tricked her into leaving. Then you broke in and stole the ball."

SOLUTION TO "THE GENIE, THE MOVIE STAR, AND THE HOBO"

Detective Bixby eyed the man her son was pointing to. "The bald guy?"

Jonah nodded. "He claims to be a bachelor living alone, and yet he bought a package of anti-snoring nose strips. If you live alone, there's no one around to tell you that you snore. My guess is his new wife,

Margo the Cat, complained about his snoring. He got to the lobby early and used the extra time to buy something to help him stop."

SOLUTION TO "AUNT PENNY'S BROOCH"

"Someone made a switch," Jonah told his mother. "Mr. Bitterman said there were a lot of copies of that brooch. It wouldn't have been hard to find one and substitute it for the real thing."

Carol Bixby thought of her two cousins. "I can't believe either Gwen or Stephanie would do that. Maybe the jeweler we went to made a mistake. Maybe it was always a fake."

"No, it was definitely switched," Jonah insisted. "The brooch was in the house all day. And yet, when I touched it just now, it was cold, like it had been outside."

"Outside?" Carol glanced over to the only new arrival, the appraiser. "You mean he brought in a fake and switched them?"

"Why not?" Jonah said. "The brooch was in the paper, so he knew what it looked like."

John Bitterman was at the door, putting on his coat, when Carol Bixby took him by the arm. "I'm sorry, Mr. Bitterman, but I'm going to have to search your pockets."

SOLUTION TO "THE DISABLED LOOKOUT"

Detective Bixby stormed into the observation room. "Jonah," she scolded her son. "Were you listening in?"

"I'm sorry," Jonah said sheepishly. "I couldn't help it."

"The whole precinct is bending the rules by letting you come here after school. You could get us all into such trouble."

"I'm sorry," Jonah said again. "But I know which guy is the look-out."

Carol Bixby paused and considered. "All right," she sighed. "I'll let it go this time. Who is it?"

"The blind guy isn't really blind," said Jonah. "When they all shook hands, he held out his left hand to the injured guy. How did he know the injured guy couldn't shake with his right?"

"Because he could see." She smiled and shook her head. "You're right. Why didn't I notice that?"

SOLUTION TO "JONAH'S NIGHTMARE"

Detective Bixby trusted her son enough to take him seriously. "What did you see? Something in the bedroom?"

"No, in the living room. He got rid of the living room rug because it was covered in blood."

"He explained that," Carol Bixby said. "They gave that rug away."

"And he was putting up a picture," Jonah added. "The house was already sold, and yet he was nailing up a new picture. Why?"

Ms. Bixby stopped in her tracks. "To cover up a bullet hole?"

"Yes!" Jonah almost shouted.

His mother thought for a moment. "Okay. I'll call Dora's niece and see if she has the rug. If not, your theory and Bob's lie might be enough to get us a search warrant. Come on."

SOLUTION TO "THE FBI AND THE HACKER"

"We're looking for the last person who used this computer, right?"

"Right," Jonah's mother confirmed. "The keyboard was wiped clean of prints, but someone used it at 7:06 this morning."

"Well, look at this." Jonah showed her the photo of Boris's computer. "The mouse pad is on the right, telling us that Boris is right-handed. But someone moved the mouse to the left side. So, the last person to use this computer must have been left-handed."

Carol thought back to her time with the students. "Oscar signed the form with his right hand," she recalled. "But when I walked into the kitchen, Mark was flipping pancakes with his left."

"Then he's your hacker," said Jonah. "He probably has his own laptop computer stashed away somewhere. It should be full of all the evidence you'll need for a conviction."

SOLUTION TO "THE LOCKED COTTAGE"

Detective Bixby looked at her son. "If it turns out to be murder, I'll call Bobby's mother and she'll pick you up. You'll still be able to play ball."

"Good," said Jonah. "I think the nephew killed her. He must've come by last night for dinner. That's when he drugged her cocoa mix."

"And how did he lock up the house from the inside?"

"He didn't. He left and Ms. Plinkov did her regular routine. She locked up, sat in front of the fire, drank her cocoa, and went to sleep. But the nephew was waiting outside. He went to the gas valve on the side of the house and turned it off. That made the fire go out. A minute later, he turned the gas back on."

Carol Bixby smiled. "That's very clever. With any luck, we'll be able to lift his prints from the gas valve. But what makes you say it's the nephew and not the niece?"

"Because the nephew was scratching his arms. It looks like poison ivy—from the poison ivy bush right next to the valve."

SOLUTION TO "THE VAMPIRE ON THE BALCONY"

Jonah led his mother and the three costumed suspects into the kitchen. He opened the drawers one by one and rummaged around. "What are you looking for, Sherlock?" asked the zombie.

"A corkscrew," Jonah answered.

"It's in the victim, honey," said his mother, a little embarrassed.

"I know that," said Jonah. "I was looking for another one."

"There isn't another one," said the gypsy. "This is a corporate apartment. They furnished it with a bare minimum of essentials."

"Then we have a problem," replied Jonah. "Because at the same time you were opening a bottle of wine, Mr. Horner says he saw the corkscrew in Mr. Jericho's chest."

The gypsy thought. "He's right. How could that be?"

"It couldn't," said Carol. "Mr. Horner, you lied about seeing the body on the balcony. Why?"

Horner didn't answer, but Jonah did. "To make us think that Mr. Jericho was dead before he arrived. He was trying to give himself an alibi. Mr. Horner is the killer."

SOLUTION TO "A TEST FOR ROOKIES"

Jonah didn't like being put on the spot. True, he had been paying close attention. These play-acting sessions were always fun. But someday he knew his mother would put him on the spot and he wouldn't have the answer.

Today wasn't that day.

Jonah put aside his geography homework and walked toward the mirror. "Mr. Pauling," he said into one of the microphones. "Can you show us exactly how you were stabbed?"

Detective Pauling walked up to the mirror. He bent over his pant leg and showed them the bloody hole. Behind the torn fabric was just a glimpse of the fake wound. Most of it was higher up on his leg. The rookies all noted the difference.

"When a person stands up, his pants move lower down on the leg," Jonah explained. "That wound was obviously made when you were sitting down. It was self-inflicted."

"Perfect," said Detective Pauling as he sat back down in the folding chair. Once again, the bloody gash became aligned with the hole in his pants, and he reached in and tore off the fake plastic wound.

SOLUTION TO "DEATH AT THE DOOR"

Carol Bixby was used to her son's clever theories, but now and then even she got exasperated. "How could you possibly know? There are no clues. No suspects, unless you count the mailman. And no prints."

"That's the clue," Jonah said, "the fact that there are no prints."

"Of course. The killer wiped them off."

"He also wiped them from the coffeemaker and the TV remote."

Carol frowned. "You're right. That is a little weird."

"Here's a good question," Jonah said. "What would you think if you'd found her husband's prints on the coffeemaker?"

"Well…" His mother thought. "I'd think the doctor was lying about his alibi. He said that his wife always made coffee after he left the house. So her prints should be on it, not his."

Jonah nodded. "I think he killed her before he left for work this morning. He set the stage by making the coffee, turning on the TV, all of that. Then he wiped off his prints. He had to."

"That would explain it." Carol smiled. "I guess I need to talk to Dr. Morton about his wife."

SOLUTION TO "FRANKIE AND THE TELESCOPE"

"What?" Frankie looked like he was ready to punch Jonah in the face.

Jonah stepped back. "Frankie, tell me something. Why do you have a jacket on?"

"Um…" Frankie didn't seem to have an answer. "Because I feel like it."

"It's the hottest day of the year," Jonah continued, "and yet you put on a jacket before coming outside."

Sally scrunched up her forehead. "You lost me, Jonah. Wearing a jacket proves that he stole my telescope?"

"Well, it proves he was outside this morning and walked across the vacant lot. That makes him a liar and a prime suspect."

"How do you figure that?" Frankie said. He folded his arms and winced a little as he did it.

"You're hiding something," Jonah said. "That's why you put on a jacket before talking to us. And I think what you're hiding is a hornet sting."

"You got stung." Sally broke out laughing. "You tried to steal my telescope and you got stung." And then, just for good measure, she punched him on the arm.

"Ow!" Frankie doubled over in pain. "I got stung three times, all right? Go take back your stupid telescope. It's nothing but trouble."

SOLUTION TO "A SUICIDAL MURDER"

Jonah picked up the suicide note and pointed out two words. "It says 'little brother' here. But it should say 'big brother.' Teddy was older than Simon. Right?"

"Yes." Carol studied the note again. "That's weird."

"Well, what if Teddy didn't kill Simon? What if it was just the opposite? What if Simon was planning to kill Teddy? He writes a suicide note, trying to mimic Teddy's handwriting. Then he leans out the window and unscrews the safety bars.

He's getting ready for when Teddy comes home from work. But Simon loses his balance and falls. An accident. Simon is not only the victim—he's also the killer."

"What about the evidence?" Carol protested. "Teddy's prints on the screwdriver?"

"A household screwdriver. Both of them used it. They both had million-dollar insurance policies. And if you're planning to kill your brother, you'd probably be moody and distracted, too."

"It makes sense," Carol said reluctantly. "I guess we were looking at the wrong brother."

SOLUTION TO "ONE DROP OF BLOOD"

"Whatever it is," Fred warned the young detective, "don't touch it. That might contaminate the chain of evidence."

"I know," said Jonah, insulted at the idea. He wasn't a child. "When Ms. Washington got here, it was daytime, right?"

"Yeah. She must have been killed between noon and 2 P.M."

"And when Mr. Hart came back to clean up the blood and DNA, it was night."

Fred thought carefully. "The security camera saw him come back around 8 P.M."

"So, the first thing he probably did was turn on the lights." Jonah pointed to the sliding dimmer switch. "So...if you slide the switch down to the off position..."

Fred grabbed an evidence vial and tore open a swab. Then he held his breath and slowly slid the dimmer down. "Oh, wow." There, in the center of the newly exposed piece of white plastic, was the tiniest drop of blood. "We got him!"

SOLUTION TO "THE SECRET LETTERS"

A curious crowd was already gathering around the old desk when Detective Bixby leaned down to her son. "How do you know the letters are forgeries?" she asked. "Is it something about the desk? Or the handwriting? Or the postage stamps?"

"No," Jonah had to admit. "I don't know anything about desks or Winston Churchill or stamps. And I don't know for sure that the letters are forgeries."

"So, what exactly do you know?"

"All I know is that there's dust on them."

"Of course there's dust," Carol said, trying to be patient. "They've been sitting around for decades."

"I know," said Jonah. "But dust doesn't magically appear. Most dust comes from people, from dead skin. If the letters weren't covered in dust when they went into that metal box, which seems unlikely, then where did the dust come from?"

"I guess you're right. When most people think 'old' they think 'dusty,' but that's not necessarily true."

"It's not true at all," Jonah said. "Someone must have planted dust on those letters, someone who wants people to think they're really old."

SOLUTION TO "UNDERCOVER JONAH"

"It's the protestor guy who was just here," Jonah told his mother. "Rhett Aronson."

"What makes you say that?" Carol asked. "Is it his shoes? You know, Jonah, a lot of animal-rights people don't wear leather. Just because Mr. Aronson looks like the obvious choice and is wearing different shoes…"

"No," Jonah said, "it's not that. It's his ticket. When we came in tonight, they tore everyone's ticket. But Mr. Aronson's ticket is still long and rectangular. It wasn't torn. That means he didn't come through the main entrance. He couldn't have. He came through the broken window."

Carol Bixby thought for a moment. "You're absolutely right. Aronson knew he'd be a suspect, so he had to have a ticket to show us. But he neglected to tear off the stub. Good job."

SOLUTION TO "THE DYING CLUE"

Carol Bixby found Jonah at her desk, playing with the Identi-Suspect software on her computer. "Jonah, that's not a video game," she scolded.

"Sorry, Mom."

"I know I've been working too much," Carol said, feeling more than a little guilty. "But I can take tomorrow off if we solve a murder tonight. You up for it?"

Jonah was always up for a good puzzle. He listened as his mother outlined the case, then sat and thought. "Why wasn't there any blood on the wallet?"

Carol frowned. "Do you think robbery was the motive after all?"

"Well, it would explain the scissors and the wallet and why Mr. Kramer was killed in Mr. Martinez's office."

"It would?"

"Sure. Larry was already in the building, delivering packages. Let's say he entered their office. It seemed empty. He looked down the hall, saw a wallet, and went to steal it. But just then Mr. Kramer walked in, bringing back the scissors he borrowed earlier that morning. They fought and Mr. Kramer got stabbed.

"Now Larry was in real trouble. He needed to blame someone. He assumed that the guy fighting for the wallet was Mr. Martinez, the guy whose name was on the door."

"You mean he got their names wrong?"

"Yeah. That's why he wrote 'Doug' in blood, trying to blame the guy's partner. Then he wiped his fingerprints off the wallet and went out to his truck. When Mona saw him, he was pretending that he'd just come back with their package."

Carol had to admit it made sense. "Larry could also have changed shirts in his truck, to get rid of the blood." She smiled. "I think you've just earned us a day off."

SOLUTION TO "WHO TOOK THE TIP?"

The homeowner looked quizzically at the twelve-year-old. "What do you mean you're a detective?"

"I mean my mom's a police detective. You can ask anyone at the Fifth Precinct. I'm good at noticing things."

The man grinned, not sure whether to believe him or not. "And what did you notice, young man?"

"I noticed that Frankie knew where your bathroom was."

The homeowner's grin faded into a frown. "You're right."

"There are three hallways and maybe a dozen doors," Jonah said, pointing out all the possible options. "But he knew exactly where it was."

"Which means he's been in this house before."

A few seconds later, Frankie emerged from the bathroom, looking calm and greatly relieved—until he saw the expression on Jonah's face.

SOLUTION TO "THE BURNING BUNGALOW"

Jonah didn't want to be glib. After all, a woman had just been carried out in a body bag. It was a sobering moment, even for a kid who was sort of used to it.

"Ms. Simmons died on the carpet, right?" he asked. "On the unburned part?"

"That's right," Detective Bixby said. "Most people collapse and die from smoke before the fire even gets to them."

"I know," Jonah replied. "But the neighbor said something different. He said the floor was already on fire when Ms. Simmons ran back in. But that has to be a lie, because the carpet underneath her body wasn't even singed."

"You're saying she was dead on the carpet before the fire started?"

"It looks that way," said Jonah.

Within twenty-four hours, they had a confession from Billy Borenson. He had heard Sarah fighting with her boyfriend that morning. After the boyfriend left, Billy came over and tried his best to become Sarah's new boyfriend. When she laughed at him, Billy lost his temper and hit her. He claimed her death was an accident, but his attempt to cover it up with an arson fire just made things worse.

ABOUT THE AUTHOR

Hy Conrad is an Edgar-nominated mystery writer who began his career as a New York playwright.

Hy has developed numerous games for Parker Brothers and Milton-Bradley, as well as computer-based mysteries. During the late 1990s, he was the creative director of Mysterynet, the largest Web site devoted to the mystery genre.

For the past six years, he has been writing and producing the TV detective series *Monk*. This is Hy's ninth book of short mysteries published by Sterling.